Sausage and Biscuit

Betsy Beacham Sceiford

Illustrated by Lynette Straite

Archway Publishing books may be ordered through booksellers or by contacting:

Archway Publishing
1663 Liberty Drive
Bloomington, IN 47403
www.archwaypublishing.com
1 (888) 242-5904

ISBN: 978-1-4808-6925-7 (sc)
ISBN: 978-1-4808-6924-0 (hc)
ISBN: 978-1-4808-6926-4 (e)

Print information available on the last page.

Archway Publishing rev. date: 11/16/2018

This book is dedicated to my wonderful grandchildren: Leah, Grant, Wiley, Etta, Thomas, Frederick, and all my future grandchildren. They are the joy of my life.

Introduction

"George, I really want a dog."
"Betsy, we don't need a dog; we like to travel."

Sausage and Buscuit

Prologue

Sausage, let me tell you the story of how I, Biscuit, came to live with our mom and dad. We had lots of fun and scary times too. First, though, I want to teach you lessons that will help you in your new life with Mom and Dad and me.

Chapter 1-Biscuit

Lesson 1: There is a human for every dog.

At Sunrise Kennels, I was very sad. All the pups from my cage were chosen by their humans. Sure, humans came to the kennel and patted my head, but I could tell I was not special to them. I wanted my very own human, but no human chose me. So I was left alone in my cage.

Then one day I heard a voice in the next room. A human was looking at the other pups.

She said, "Not this one. It is too big. Not this one either. It is too rough. No, that girl puppy hiding under the table is too shy."

Then the human looked at me. I was sitting in the doorway. She smiled. I was smiling inside. I liked her voice. I loved her smell. I wanted to be nearer to her. She was here for me—I just knew it. I thought, *Please let her hold me. Please let her want me.* I ran into the room and jumped up to her. She picked me up. I could tell she loved me already. Oh, Sausage, I was really happy! I had picked her, and she had picked me. We left together.

Outside, the smells were amazing, and the air was cool and clean. We got into a car, and it began to move. I got to sit on my human's lap. She patted me, hugged me, and told me I was soft, wonderful, and cute. Of course, I knew that already! Then—oops! I threw up all over her. What a mess! She loved me anyway.

Lesson 2: There is a pack for everyone.

My human said my name was Biscuit. She called herself Mom. She said, "Mom loves you, Biscuit." I loved her too. She was comfy and warm, so I slept a long time. After a while, the car stopped, and we got out in cold, white stuff Mom called snow.

I stepped into the snow, and Mom said, "Go potty!" The snow was cold, so I peed right away. When I did, she jumped around clapping and smiling, so I guessed it was all good.

Soon, another car drove up. In it was a big human called George. I was a little afraid of him. More snow was coming down. Then Mom put me into the car with George. She said that she was going to get her suitcase. I was nervous without her.

Soon, Mom came back. She opened the car door and looked in. What did she see? I was gone! "Where's my Biscuit?" Mom asked. "George, where is my puppy? Did you throw him out the door?"

"Certainly did," George answered.

Mom believed him right away because she knew that George didn't want Mom to get a puppy. She thought that George had thrown me into the snow. She was mad! Then George smiled and opened his warm coat. I was cuddled up all warm and comfy inside his coat. She reached for me to put me onto her lap. Dad said in a kind voice, "No, Biscuit is fine right here with me. I am Dad, Biscuit. You can ride home right where you are."

So we drove happily home together. All the way, I was wondering what my new home would be like.

When we arrived, I got to jump around in the snow again. I was eight weeks old, and I weighed three pounds. I was very little but very fast. But soon they caught me, and they fed me in my own new bowl. Then they tucked me into a crate with my own blanket, which Mom had brought from my old home at Sunrise Kennels. I was very tired, so I flopped down and went right to sleep. Mom came down and took me outside twice to pee. She said I was a great pup, so I was happy, but she looked sleepy. Poor Mom needed more rest!

The next morning when I woke up, I let my new mom and dad give me toys, and we played together. It was great fun! Then I took Mom for a walk around the neighborhood. Actually, I had her carry me. What an adventure! I saw lots of birds and cars. Many people saw me and noticed how cute I was. Mom was proud to show off such a good pup. When we got back, I slept for hours. When I woke up, Mom played with me again. She gave me special treats, which I gobbled up right away. I liked them, and I realized that I loved my humans too.

Lesson 3: Know who the alpha is.

Several weeks went by, and I learned that my mom was in charge in our house. Dogs like to be together in groups called packs, and the leader is called the alpha. Mom was our alpha. She flipped me over and told me that. She wanted to be sure that I knew who was boss.

For a few weeks, I had to sleep alone in my crate. Why was I down here without my pack? Finally Mom let me come upstairs. I wanted to sleep as close to the alpha as possible. I tried to sleep on Mom's head or her pillow, but she moved me to the bottom of the bed. Sometimes, though, I snuck up onto her pillow anyway.

Months passed. Mom and I went for many walks. She used a long string called a leash to keep me from running away as fast as a rabbit. In fact, it was a rabbit I wanted to chase. Actually, I wanted to chase cars and birds and anything that moved. When we got home, I climbed up our hill and was proud to pee by lifting my leg for the first time. I had figured out that boy dogs lift their legs when they pee. It was not so hard, but I lifted the wrong leg and ended up rolling down the hill. Mom laughed. I did not think it was funny.

Lesson 4: Protect your pack.

When I got bigger, Mom let me stay on a long leash near her while she was working in the garden. I loved chasing birds and barking at one big one that Mom said was called a bald eagle. She said there was a nest of bald eagles near our house by the lake. That day, the eagle spotted me right away. He started flying around in circles above me. He looked big, and there were long claws on his feet. I stood on my back legs and hopped up and down to scare him away. I decided I would protect Mom from that big eagle.

But the eagle didn't go away. He stayed high up in the air and flew around and around me. I barked louder so that he would know I was the boss. Then he swooped down with his claws out. I growled and barked; then I leaped into the air, and the eagle got closer. Still I was not afraid, but Mom was! My barking had gotten her attention. She screamed loudly and flapped her arms around in the air. I protected her by barking and jumping. I scared him off! My mom's yelling scared him off too. We had protected each other.

One day Dad tried to protect me too. He was outside fixing his boat. He looked up and saw a white dog zipping by on our road. Right away, he ran after it. He raced down the road yelling, "Stupid dog!" and other words I did not know. "You could get run over, Biscuit. You are not allowed to run free in the road. You could get hurt. Why don't you listen?" Dad sounded mad, but I knew he was trying to protect his little dog. He didn't want a car to hit me.

Then something funny happened. A lady came out onto her porch and asked Dad why he was chasing *her* dog. Dad explained that he was chasing his own dog. Certainly, he knew what his own dog looked like. After all, the dog had lived with him for months.

"Hmm," said the woman. "My dog is a girl pup. Shall we check?"

Oops, my dad had been wrong! Dad hurried home to find Mom and me playing on the front deck. We'd been watching Dad chase the other white dog, and we thought it was very

funny! But we knew that my dad was trying to protect me because we are in the same pack.

Later, Mom took me to meet the nice lady with the white dog. Her name was Bethany, and her white puppy's name was Vera. I really liked Vera. She became my friend and even came to my first birthday party. We had lots of playdates together after that. Sometimes protecting the pack can lead to a nice surprise.

Lesson 5: When you gotta go … get to the side of the road.

One sunny day, we went on another walk along the road by the lake. I liked to walk down the middle of the road, so I could see more birds. Also, everyone could see me! On this day I needed to take a poop, right there in the middle of the road, my favorite place. Mom was upset because a car had been waiting behind us for a long time. It wanted to drive down the road, but I was right in the middle, doing my business. Mom bent down to pick it up with a plastic bag (Mom treasured all my gifts), and she told the driver of the car that she was sorry we had made her wait.

The car moved slowly by, and the driver rolled down the window. She smiled and said, "When you gotta go, you've gotta go!"

I agreed with her, but Mom just laughed and herded me over to the side of the road.

Lesson 6: Help with chores.

One day when we were at home, I wanted to help Mom with the dishwasher. I stood on the door to hold it down and licked the plates for her. She kept moving me off. "Biscuit," she scolded, "get off of my dishwasher! You will break it!" That made it much harder to help.

Next, I helped with the laundry. I fell into the basket and looked things over with my sharp eyes. I found a pair of Mom's underpants. I pulled them from the basket, and with my head held high, I carried them into the family room, where Mom and her book club friends were discussing their monthly book. Then Mom and I played tug-of-war with her underpants. I seemed to enjoy it more than she did.

Lesson 7: Have a way out.

Sausage, I trained my humans to let me out when I rang the cowbell on the front door. I would go out to pee and then I would come back in and get a treat. I am smart, so I decided to ring the bell a lot just to get more treats. But they were not so easily fooled. They only gave me treats when I really had done my business.

Lesson 8: More is sometimes better.

I heard Dad say, "Betsy, you wanted a dog, but I really needed a dog!"

That's great for me because I am the dog they loved and needed.

Saucy, sometimes I was still lonely when Mom and Dad would go away for hours. I missed my humans! I wished I could have playdates, but no one came with their dogs, so I was home alone. I heard Dad tell Mom how I pouted when she was not here. He noticed how I waited by the door until she arrived. Why did she not just stay home and play with me all the time? Dad could stay and play too.

I heard Mom and Dad talking.

Mom said, "George, I think Biscuit would enjoy having another dog live here with us. Maybe an older dog, his size, but trained. What do you think?"

"Betsy, I have been thinking we should get another puppy. They could play together, and we each would have a dog to hold. I love puppies."

"Hmmm. So, George, who would get up at night to train this new puppy?"

"You, naturally!" Dad laughed. "Let's go look at some puppies and then decide."

Dad drove Mom and me to Sunrise Kennel. A playdate—yay! Wow, there were a lot of pups. It was a blast! Mom liked you, Saucy, since you were friendly and a beautiful brown. You liked me and jumped all over me. She also liked the white-and-gray one who was your sister. You ganged up on me, and I jumped up onto a chair. You chased me, but I was bigger and got away! Ha, You did not know how fast I was. I wanted to come back for more playdates!

It was fun, but I was tired and ready to take my humans home. Then Mom carried the brown pup and the gray one outside to meet Dad. I thought it was nice of her to include Dad and extend our playdate. I heard her say, "I love the brown-colored one, George. I will call her Sausage, and the gray one can be Gravy."

Dad replied, "You are crazy. Pick one, and let's go." Mom picked You!

Now I wondered why you, Sausage, had joined us in the car. Were you coming for a visit? Naturally, Mom held me on her lap, and you were put in a carrier in the back seat. You cried and whined and were a big pain. Soon Mom let you come up front too. It was okay. I could share her lap for a little while.

Chapter 2-Sausage: Beginnings

I loved playing in the big room with all the pups at Sunrise Kennels. My sister and I liked the new big white dog that came to play. The human who brought the white dog picked me up and said that I was very soft. She loved my brown colors. She also picked up my sister and took us to meet a large human. He liked us both, but I was the only one put in the big car.

Wait! I thought. *What about my sister?* I whimpered and cried because I didn't want to leave, and I was alone in the back of this car in a stupid carrier. The lady human told me the white dog was called Biscuit and that my new name was Sausage—Saucy, for short. I liked that. I have always been saucy. She said to call her Mom and the big human Dad. I wondered why Biscuit got to sit up front with Mom while I was in the back seat.

I wanted to sit up front with her too. I liked her smell. I also liked the scent that meant she had treats. We stopped for a break. Mom said I rode very well in the car. She was glad I did not throw up. Why would I do that? Then she brought me up front. Biscuit and I both slept in her lap. Finally we got to a house. I peed in the yard, and boy, was Mom excited and happy. You would think she had never seen a dog pee before this, and yet she already had a dog taking care of her.

I liked Biscuit. We began playing as soon as we got into the house. I took a toy away from him and let him know who was boss. They fed us, and Biscuit stood back and let me eat first. I might weigh three pounds and be ten weeks old, but Mom said, "Wow, she is the lead pup." She also said she, Mom, was in charge. Mom flipped me upside down and read me the riot act. I guess she was the alpha of the pack, all right, but I planned to be her beta. Every pack always had an alpha and a beta who was second in charge and the alpha's best helper.

Dad held me and threw toys for me. He was fun. But I was put in a crate for the night. Mom gave me a soft blanket from my old kennel, but Biscuit got to go upstairs with them. I cried and whimpered, but it did no good. Maybe I was not important. I was so lonely and very sad. I thought maybe I was a bad pup.

In the middle of the night, Mom came down, followed by Biscuit, so we could go out to pee. Mom jumped around and said, "Good Sausage." But back I went into the crate again. They went upstairs without me. Didn't they know I wanted to be an important part of the pack? I was the beta!

Nights went by like this for a while, and then, at last, Mom invited me to come upstairs. She lifted me onto the bed, and I tried to sleep on her pillow. She said, "No way!" She was still the alpha. I snuck up on her pillow when she was asleep and so did Biscuit!

I woke her up early with licks on her face. We went out, did our thing, and went back to

sleep. At last I was an important member of my new pack. I slept by the alpha, protecting her. Mom took me to a place she called the vet. The doctor lady gave me pinches by my neck and in my bottom. Mom said it was good for me and that she had brought Biscuit here too. The vet lady gave me a treat and said, "Good puppy." I guess it was okay.

I was now helping with loading the dishwasher and sorting the clothes. I also played tug-of-war with Biscuit using Mom's underpants. This was the life!

Biscuit: Time together

I wondered, *When is this playdate ending?*

When Sausage sat on Dad's lap, I jumped up and sat on him too. I wanted every toy Saucy had, and she wanted every toy, bone, or bit of food I had too. And she took them from me! What was with that? Mom explained that her heart was big and that it grew even bigger when Saucy came to stay. She said that there was plenty of love for both of us.

On the plus side, Saucy was fun to wrestle with and chase all over the house. She followed me everywhere. She threw small balls into the air with her nose, and we chased them together. I got into Mom's knitting bag, and we dragged the yarn all over the house. Mom yelled, "No, no!" and jumped around gathering up the yarn. She was pretty upset, but we thought it was great fun!

Even though I was jealous of Saucy at first, I believed Mom when she told me that she and Dad had room in their hearts for each of us. I began to realize that Sausage was staying forever, and then I was glad. We did everything together, and we always had fun. I decided that I would let myself love her. We were a family as well as a pack.

Sausage: Time apart

One beautiful day, Mom put us out in the yard to run inside the invisible fence. Invisible fences are sort of magical. You can't see them, but if you try to cross them, they give you a little shock in your collar. The shock reminds you to stay in the yard where it is safe.

That day, Biscuit and I had our special collars on so we could run and be free to play. I was sniffing around the yard when I heard Mom's voice. The window was open, and her words floated out to me.

"George, I don't see Biscuit out in the yard. Saucy is there, but she's not playing with him. I'll go check on them." She appeared at the door and called to me, "Saucy, where is Biscuit?"

I glimpsed Biscuit's collar lying on the ground near the big tree. I ran over to it, sniffed it, and barked until Mom came over and picked it up to examine it. She did not understand how it could have fallen off. She told me not to worry; Biscuit would come back soon. Whenever he got loose, he always came back home.

But this time Biscuit did not come back. I was so sad. I hadn't seen Biscuit leave the yard; I had been sniffing a dead tree. *Where are you, Biscuit?* I thought. *I need my buddy! I miss you! Come home soon. I am very lonely.*

Mom, Dad, and I walked all around the neighborhood. Then we drove everywhere. Mom cried. Dad was so sad. I was the saddest of all! That night was awful. Biscuit was not with us.

We had lost a member of our pack. We posted pictures of Biscuit all over town, and Mom called on all her Facebook humans to help her (whatever that means). Weeks went by, and I was so unhappy. I was a Sausage without my Biscuit.

I wondered, *Does he miss me? Is he hurt?* We continued to drive around town and out into the countryside to look for Biscuit. We looked for him every day. Sometimes we saw white dogs we thought were Biscuit, but they weren't.

Finally, on our last trip far out in the countryside, Dad spotted a dog that looked just like Biscuit. This dog was tied to a long line and looked very sad. When I saw him, I barked and whined, and Dad stopped the car. Mom jumped out and ran to the dog. She hugged him, and they rolled around on the grass together (which was not so easy for Mom). The dog licked her face and was so very happy. This was our Biscuit! I just knew it!

Then I saw a man come out of the house. Mom got up fast. He yelled at Mom! Dad and I got out of the car and stood nearby to help. The man said, "I am Frank! What are you doing with my dog?"

Mom answered him, "This is our dog, Biscuit! Oh, why is this new red collar on him?"

Frank yelled, "He's my dog, Snowball. Now get off my property! I've had him a long time. If you don't leave, I'll call the police."

Mom answered, "Go ahead. Call the police. Call them now."

Chapter 3 Biscuit

I was so happy! Mom had found me. My special human was here at last! Dad and Sausage were here too. What was the holdup? I thought, *Put me in our car. Let me sleep on Mom's lap. Let me lick dad and play with Saucy.* The man was mean. Since I'd been at his house, he had given me almost no food and not much water either. He never gave me treats. I was hungry! I was left outside almost all day and all night too. I didn't like being at Frank's house. I wanted to go home with Mom, Dad, and Saucy. But I smelled some meat in Frank's pocket; maybe he was finally going to feed me.

Then Mom said the police were here. I thought the man was saying that I was his dog. Ha!

No way! Maybe I was thinner because I didn't get enough to eat, but I was still Biscuit. Dad and Mom explained to the police that I was their dog. One police officer picked me up and put me halfway between Mom and the man, Frank. He told them to call the dog. Mom called, "Here, Biscuit!"

The man called, "Here, Snowball."

I thought, *Well, I've already greeted Mom, and the man does have yummy-smelling meat in his pocket.* I went to the man. I knew Mom would want me to get a treat. Sausage went to the man too. We ripped his pocket to get to our treat while he screamed.

Dad yelled that Frank cheated by having food in his pocket. Mom said in her very sternest voice, "Come, Biscuit Come Sausage!"

We turned to go to her, but the man grabbed me. "This is my dog, Snowball," he yelled.

Ha, I was not some silly Snowball. My name was Biscuit.

"Possession is nine-tenths of the law," Frank said.

"Not in this case," said Dad calmly. "We have pictures of both dogs from the time when they were just little pups."

Frank answered, "That's just a pup that looks like Snowball. That is no proof. You tried to steal him. I'm sorry, but he is mine."

Then Mom spoke up. Looking very confident, she said, "You are not sorry, but you will be. Officers, I had an identification chip put in both pups in case they got lost. Biscuit is registered with North East Hometown Veterinary Hospital. Check it out with them."

I'm not sure whether the police officer called the vet's office, but when Frank learned that I had a chip, he gave in and admitted I wasn't his dog.

The police officer gave me to Mom and left, warning Frank that he should have told the truth. We could press charges.

"Okay," said Frank, "you're right. I found him by the side of the road. But I am lonely. I want to keep him."

Frank must have thought that Mom would feel sorry for him because he was alone. He said, "Look, I saw you had two dogs, and I was nice and left you the little brown jumpy one, didn't I? Could you not let me have the white one?"

Mom answered," I knew it! You took Biscuit's collar off and stole him. Before you go get a dog, realize you must feed him well, have bowls of water for him, play with him, and love him a lot. And then and only then, go and adopt a dog. Don't take someone else's beloved pet. Biscuit is an important member of our family, and we are taking him home with us."

Frank hung his head because he knew he had done a bad thing. I really only cared that I was going home to be with my family. I had missed them. We got into the car and drove off together. We were happy; we were going home.

Biscuit
Lesson 9: Love is the most important thing!

Sausage, I have one final lesson to explain to you. You may already have figured it out from some of the earlier lessons, but I want to end with it because it really is the most important.

This lesson is about love. Love is what holds us together as a family. We weren't born a family, after all. You and I are dogs, and Mom and Dad are humans. That doesn't matter, though, because our love glues us together into a family.

When you first came to live with us, I was jealous of you. You were little and cute, and you still had that lovely puppy smell. Mom and Dad fussed over you and cuddled you, and I thought that they were ignoring me. I thought that they had only a certain amount of love, and I didn't want them to give it to you; I wanted it for myself. I wanted you to go back to

Sunrise Kennels and stay there. I wanted to be the center of Mom and Dad's love as I was before you arrived.

Now I know that I was wrong. Love just keeps getting bigger and bigger when there are more people or more dogs to love. Love can get so big, in fact, that there is no end to it! It grows and grows and grows until it spreads out all over the whole family. There's even enough to share with people and dogs outside the family.

When you, dad, and mom rescued me from Frank, I came home to our family and felt wonderful. I was in my right place, and I could feel Mom and Dad's love—and yours! I was happy. We went back to doing the fun things we had done before: we took long walks in the neighborhood and visited all our regular doggy friends—Nikki, Rusty, and Charlie. We had playdates with Vera, Tucker, and Calvin. We searched for underpants and knitting yarn and brought our toys to play with Mom and Dad. Life was normal once more.

But I would never be the same again. I had grown up. I had learned a valuable lesson about what really matters. Love really matters, Saucy. I know that now. Love is the very most important thing!

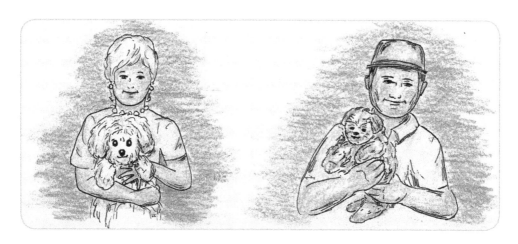

Acknowledgements

Many people have helped me to write this book. I especially want to thank George Teribery, who did not want a dog but realized he needed not one but two dogs. He has loved and helped care for Biscuit and Sausage. He is certainly a member of our special pack.

Next, I wish to thank my very talented illustrator, Lynette Straite. For years we talked in the teacher's faculty rooms about writing and illustrating a book together. At last our dream is coming true.

I must acknowledge my parents who read to my sister, Barbara, and me every night as we grew up. Mom told me made-up stories that lit the imagination and fueled the desire to make up my own.

Thank you to the Erie Day School, where I learned to enjoy exciting literature and developed writing and grammar skills that have assisted me throughout my life.

I appreciate Daniel and Amanda Steeneck, who heard and read this manuscript multiple times. They offered many ideas and endless encouragement.

I acknowledge the editing assistance and many suggestions of Pamela Blair and Linda Rich, who read this book at our college reunion. I also thank Pam Vergona, a former reading recovery teacher leader who helped me level the book. Thank you to a special friend, Lynda Semelka, who was the first person to read *Sausage and Biscuit*. Her laughter and encouragement kept me going when I was the most unsure of myself. Thank you to my sister, Barbara Anderson, who called every morning to ask about my progress.

Thank you to Emily Northway, who assisted with formatting and printing out working copies of the book multiple times. I also am grateful to Beth Blackburn, who took the picture of the author and her pups. She also helped to format the illustrations used in this book.

I most especially want to thank Sausage and Biscuit. Without these wonderful dogs, there would be no book. They bring such joy and laughter into my life and the lives of others.

Biscuit and Sausage are Havanese dogs. Their ancestors were bred in Cuba from the Bichon family. They adapted to the climate becoming smaller dogs with long silky hair (though some are curly). Most are 10 pounds and are eight to ten inches high. They are happy sociable dogs and adaptable but do not like long absences from their family. They adore kids and adults and are very smart. They like to bark and must be taught early to quit barking on command. They are curious and love to sit high up on the back of a chair to see what's going on nearby. They are sensitive and don't respond well when yelled at by their owners. Daily walks and play will be enough to keep Havanese pups healthy and happy. This breed is great for those that are allergic because they do not shed and are considered non-allergenic.

TIPS

1. My dogs will eat anything that even looks slightly edible. Keep them away from chocolate and grapes. Both can make them very ill. Get rid of or avoid any mushrooms in the yard or on your walks. Call your vet right away if eaten.

2. Many dog's noses turn very pink when eating from a plastic dish. Biscuits did. I switched to a stainless-steel bowls and after several months, his nose became shiny black again.

3. Housebreaking can be difficult for small dogs. Ours still have occasional accidents. I like crate training and recommend going on many outdoor walks during their waking hours.

4. Be ready to have your dog follow you wherever you go (even the bathroom!). Pat them, love them, and they will return that love three-fold.

About the Illustrator

Lynette has enjoyed doing artwork since she was a small child. So, becoming an elementary art teacher was a natural choice for her.

She now shares her love of art and her Christian faith while doing chalk art programs and teaching others this art form.

She also enjoys her roles of mom and grandma in her Pennsylvania home.

CPSIA information can be obtained
at www.ICGtesting.com
Printed in the USA
BVHW020256021218
534468BV00003B/3/P